FOSSIL FAMILY TALES

BETWEEN FRIENDS

For Elliot – K.G.

For Sam – S.M.

Text Copyright © 1992 by Kate Green
Illustrations Copyright © 1992 by Steve Mark
Published by The Child's World, Inc.
123 South Broad Street, Mankato, Minnesota 56001
All Rights Reserved. No form of this book may be
reproduced or transmitted in any form or by any means,
electronic or mechanical, including photocopying,
recording, or by an information storage and retrieval system
without express permission in writing from the publisher.
Printed in the United States of America.

Distributed to schools and libraries
in the United States by
ENCYCLOPAEDIA BRITANNICA EDUCATIONAL CORP.
310 South Michigan, Ave.
Chicago, Illinois 60604

Library of Congress Cataloging-in-Publication Data

Green, Kate,
   Between friends / story by Kate Green; illustrated by Steve Mark.
   p. cm.
   Summary: Little dinosaur Buddy Rocks suffers from the thoughtless bullying and careless violence of big Rex, until Buddy sets certain boundaries and tells Rex what he expects from their relationship.
   ISBN 0-89565-780-5
   [1. Dinosaurs – Fiction.   2. Bullies – Fiction.   3. Friendship – Fiction.
4. Interpersonal relations – Fiction.]   I. Mark, Steve, ill.   II. Title.
PZ7.G82354Be   1992
[E] – dc20   91-32706
                                                                  CIP
                                                                  AC

BETWEEN FRIENDS

Setting Boundries

Story by Kate Green
Illustrations by Steve Mark

Back eons ago
before neon lights,
stars and stripes,
freeways and tv's,
lived a small dinosaur,
namely me,
Buddy Rocks.
I had spikey spines,
a fine toothy smile
and scales any reptile
could be proud of.

It was tough out there in the swampy mud-holes. Fanged mammoths stalked their prey.

Volcanoes blasted every day. Huge creatures on their way to a meal had a disturbing zeal for munching. It was an eat-or-be-eaten world.

A herd of hungry lizards
tall as ten trees –
that was my neighborhood,
if you please.
I was scared each time
some big-oaf brontosaurous
cruised my block.

And I rocked like an earthquake
when the Big Guy came my way.
He was square-nosed
and fat-necked.
Wherever he stepped
he always wrecked.
That's why we called him
Tyrant Rex.

He was mean as
his scales were green.
I didn't dare cross him.
I let him boss me around
but I didn't like it.
I just squinted my eyes up
like two sharp swords
and glanced away.
"Leave me alone!"
I wanted to say.

One day Rex rammed into my room
with a boom,
yelling, "I came to play!
Out of my way!"
He didn't care if my cave
was a special place.

He kicked my toys
all over the place
and tossed my
bone-block set around.
He tore my reptile-dolls
right down off a rock.
He drew his name
in flaming orange
across the floor.

He squashed my stone checkers, then had the nerve to heckle me some more. As he was leaving, he threw me a coconut curve-ball then stomped out like nothing mattered to him at all.

This time he'd pushed me
to the wall. He'd gone too far.
Even Rex had to have some rules.
I was tired of being
his personal stomping ground.
He just couldn't keep that up.

"Yup," I grumbled, "But still I'm scared to tell him how I feel. I'm quite a bit smaller than him." I trembled in my scaley skin.

Just then, my mother ambled along.
I told her exactly
what had gone wrong.
I said, "Rex had his mind set
on messing with me.
It was rough!"

" **Y**ou are going
to have to get tough," said she.
"You're going to have to set a
boundary
in very clear words that say
how you did not like
what he did today.
Tell him you want him
to act differently
next time. Tell Rex,
'You are not welcome
in my room
if all you do
is smash and bash my stuff.
I've had enough. Please,
respect my place.'"

I looked up at my mother's face.
"You mean," I asked,
"I have to tell Rex to stop?"
"Exactly," she said.
"Now I've got to shop
for some stone-ground plant leaves
for supper. Good luck,
little duck!" she cried.
I shivered in shock
at the thought of telling Rex
he had to stop wrecking.

The next day I had my chance.
I found Rex trampling
some flowering plants
and knocking down a fence
with his foot.
At first I thought
I should sneak by unseen,
not cause trouble.
I mean, what if I told him
and all he did was hate me?
Or worse yet,
he turned and ate me?

I pictured my boundary
as a wall of stones
no one could push down.
It would make me strong
while I told Rex
what I wanted.

Then I pictured it again,
that boundary wall.
This time it was a tall curtain of light
that would shield me.
I'd have no need to be frightened.
I'd be safe
in my right to say
just what was on my mind.

"Oh Rex," I called. I looked up a mile at his bullying smile. "I've got to set a boundary with you and I want you to respect it. You may not come to my cave to play if all you're going to do is wreck all day. If you do it once more my door is closed to you."

With that he turned and tramped off
to the swamp.

The next day he was back
at my door,
wanting to come in
and recklessly wreck some more.
In he came with a little dance.
I cringed
at the size of his footprints.
Then I took the chance to remind him,
"Oh Rex, I hope you remember what
I said to you about my favorite things."

"It rings a bell," said he.
"Try again," said me.
"You told me, 'Don't wreck it.'
Right?" Rex asked.
"You've got it.
Respect it,"
I said. I still had
a secret, sinking dread
that he was five times
bigger than me.

At first he looked nervous.
He wriggled in his giant skin
holding on tight
to my bone collection.
He carefully handled my prized
selection of dinosaur eggs.
I held my breath,
sure he'd break them.

But Rex relaxed
and placed them neatly
back in their case.
Then, with a grin,
he said, "I'm glad
you let me in.
I didn't know
that wrecking was bad.
In my family
its the only thing
that gets me
any attention."

He shyly smiled,
leaping over
all the eggs at once.
Tumbling toward me,
he tangled his legs.

He swooped
to miss squishing,
squashing,
breaking,
blasting,
thrashing,
crashing,
and crushing
the tender eggs.

Then he landed
in a heap
at my feet.

Oh my, thought I.
I'm one dead dinosaur now…

But instead,
Rex raised his massive head
and whispered, "Oops!

I do want to respect
your boundary!
I really do want you around me.
It's just that sometimes
I'm clumsy."
Gently, he nudged
a tiny egg my way.
"I tried," he said.

I sighed as I put the eggs
on a high shelf.
"Rex, I do like you
in spite of myself.
And you know what?"
I added.
"I like me better, too,
every spike and tooth,
now that I told you
the truth about
what I was feeling."

We hugged
and it was good to know
a boundary isn't a brick wall
at all.
Hearts can reach through
respectfully,
not wreck-fully!
This was the start
of a whole new
friendship.